WHERE'S SARA?

Written by

Melissa Henry

Illustrated by

Pavani Apsara

For permission requests, write the author at: wotimdfw@gmail.com

Editors: Naomi Ainsworth (Trinity Writing & Publishing), Tracy DeSimone and Emmanuel Writing Services

Formatted by: Trinity Writing and Publishing

LOUISE TRASK MEMORIAL FOUNDATION

"Where's Sara?"
was written by Melissa Henry
in the 7th grade in 1990. It is a book her
mother helped her create. Her mother,
Louise Trask, passed away in July 2021. Melissa
with her husband, Dr. Kevin E. Henry, as founders
and Pastors of Word of Truth International Ministries
in Pantego, TX, have set up a memorial foundation
in her honor. Louise Trask, a loving mother of two
children, was a survivor of domestic abuse.
The Louise Trask Memorial Foundation is set up to
assist women who have suffered domestic violence
and their children, providing funds for a deposit on a
new home. Educational funding is also available, as
Louise Trask was supportive of educational
opportunities as well.
All proceeds from this book will go directly to this
special foundation, representing "A Caring Heart" for
others! For more Information about the Louise Trask
Memorial Foundation visit: www.CFSNM.org

Mrs. Rabbit   Tanya   Courtney

Dan　　　　Peter　　　Sara　　Mr. Rabbit

Written by
Melissa Henry

Illustrated by
Pavani Apsara

Once upon a time, there was a happy, playful family of rabbits who lived in the Gila Forest. This family of rabbits lived in a burrow in the middle of the forest. Besides the Rabbit Family, there were other animals who made the forest their home. It was a pleasant place for the animals to live. When they were outside, the animals played together and had lots of fun, like one big, happy family.

The rabbit family consisted of Mr. and Mrs. Rabbit, and five three-month-old cute, cuddly bunnies. Four of the baby rabbits were mostly all gray with white spots. The runt of the litter was Sara. Sara had black fur with specks of white throughout. She inherited this coloring from her grandfather on her dad's side. Her father also inherited a little of the black fur, but not nearly as much as Sara.

Other than Sara, the rest of the bunnies consisted of two girls and two boys. The girls' names were Tanya and Courtney, and the boys were named Dan and Peter. Tanya was the most mature rabbit. She thought that family was very important. Courtney, on the other hand, was the prissy one. She hated bugs, and any slimy dirty thing she saw. Courtney spent lots of time combing her fur and looking at herself in the mirror, but she loved her family too.

The last girl bunny was Sara, who always seemed to be in her own little world. She spent lots of time playing alone or singing and never got bored. She kept busy just by counting to herself. Sara was the type of rabbit interested in everything that lived or grew in the forest. She loved insects, birds, snow, and the smell of rain during a rainstorm in the Gila Forest. She liked meeting, seeing, and finding new things while walking through the forest. Like Tanya, she loved her family and liked making new animal friends her own age.

Dan and Peter were always trying to catch bugs. They loved to study them. They were caring bunnies and never killed the bugs. Instead, they let them go after they finished observing and recording information such as their looks, size, and color. The two boys were best friends, always thinking and liking the same things.

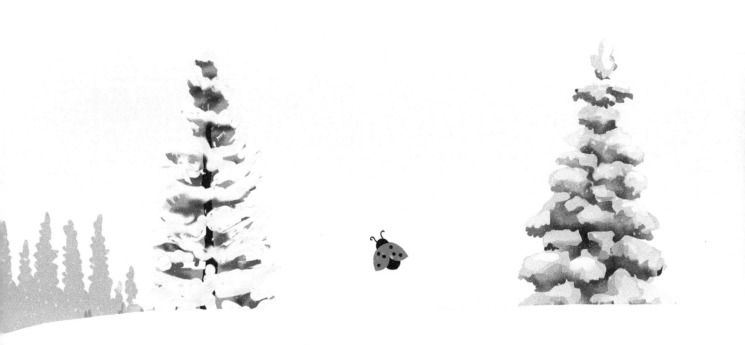

Mr. and Mrs. Rabbit were indeed good parents who cared for their baby bunnies greatly. They believed knowing how to behave and being polite were very important.

One wintery Saturday afternoon, the snow had stopped falling, and most of the animals in the forest were out playing in the snow and having lots of fun. The bunnies were in their home, finishing up their weekend cleaning.

"Mom, may we please go outside and play in the snow with everyone else?" asked Sara.

"Yeah, Mom, can we please go outside? It would be lots of fun!" added the other bunnies, with hopeful looks on their furry faces.

"Well, I don't know, let's see," Mrs. Rabbit said while pulling some lettuce out of the refrigerator. "What do you think, honey?" she asked Mr. Rabbit.

"Have they finished all of the cleaning for the weekend?" Mr. Rabbit asked as the little rabbits sat, all ears, waiting to hear what their father would say.

"Yes, Dear, they have finished. In fact, they did a mighty good job of it, too," said Mrs. Rabbit as she picked up the big, green lettuce leaf and bit off half of it.

"That's good to hear, I suppose." Before Mr. Rabbit finished the sentence, the bunnies hopped towards the front door and outside into the white snow.

"Wow!" shouted the bunnies joyfully, smiling from their foreheads to their chins. They pounced about, throwing snowballs at each other and having lots of fun.

"I've never seen anything so beautiful in my whole life!" Sara exclaimed as her eyes roamed around, looking at everything in wonderment.

"I know what you mean. I'm so thankful we are together and get to share this wonderful, lovely, amazing experience," replied Tanya as she hugged Sara and told her how much she loved her. She told Sara how thankful she was that they were sisters.

Although Sara loved her sister, she did not want to spend the rest of the afternoon listening to Tanya go on and on about the importance of family and being together, so Sara walked away as Tanya continued to rattle on to herself.

Hippidy, Hopidy....

I didn't think I'd ever lose her, thought Sara. I think family is important, but I'd like to venture out before it gets dark. Sara scurried on, not realizing she had strayed from her siblings.

It was her tendency to wander, but before she knew it, she was farther away from home than she had ever gone before.

Sara stopped and she gazed around. The forest was covered with snow. "Pretty," she exclaimed hopping around and singing, "Here comes Peter Cottontail, hopping down the bunny trail, hippity, hoppity…" Sara sang on and on until suddenly she let out a terrible scream. Sara was so busy singing and hopping she had not watched where she was going and fell into a large hole. "Bang!" Sara hit the hard bottom of the hole.

"Oww!" Sara yelped. "Where am I? What happened? The last thing I remember was hopping around and singing Peter Cottontail. I must have fallen down some sort of trap!" It was very dark in the hole, which was at least seven feet deep and so wide that even if she stretched as far as she could, she still couldn't touch both sides at once. It was definitely a man-made trap.

"Oh, what will I do? How will I ever get out of here?" Sara cried.

As small as I am, it will be impossible! I don't think any of the other animals are around to help rescue me from this awful place, she thought as tears trickled down her furry little face.

* * *

Where Am I ?

I am scared!

"What do you mean she's missing? Where did you see her last?" asked Mrs. Rabbit, with anger and concern in her voice.

"I saw her last," Tanya said tearfully. "I was talking to her earlier, and that was the last time anyone saw her. It's all my fault!" she bawled.

"No, it's not anyone's fault, so quit your crying. We don't have time for it," responded Mr. Rabbit. "We are going to form a search party, so let's get started."

Out into the snow-blanketed land they went. They split into two groups and agreed to meet back home when the moon was up.

As they began to look, they started to worry. They tried to look on the bright side, but darkness fell, and it was cold. All they could think about were the dreadful things that could happen to Sara.

The Rabbit Family was aware of the dangers that lurked deep in the otherwise peaceful forest and what kind of trouble could happen to Sara while she was all alone. It was very hard for them as they searched, hoping they would find her safe. They continued, knowing how difficult it would be to find Sara in such a large area.

When the moon was up, the family stopped searching and returned to their home, even though they had not found little Sara. The baby bunnies could hardly keep their eyes open, and even though Mr. Rabbit did not want to stop, Mrs. Rabbit convinced him the children could not stay awake any longer and must be put to bed. She also convinced him they wouldn't be able to find Sara while it was dark. Mr. Rabbit agreed it was time for them to go home and put the bunnies to bed, but they would get up the next morning and continue their search.

The bunnies fell asleep immediately, and even though Sara's parents were tired, they could not fall asleep. Both lay in bed worrying about Sara.

Eventually, Mr. and Mrs. Rabbit fell asleep, but it seemed they only slept for an hour all night.

They were all awake at five a.m. and ready for a long day looking for their lost Sara.

Mr. and Mrs. Rabbit knew they needed to find Sara sooner rather than later. She had already been alone all night long.

Mrs. Rabbit fixed breakfast and told the young ones to eat quickly so they could get an early start. They had a long, hard day ahead of them. The children ate their breakfast salad and gulped down their water.

"We're ready, Mom and Dad," said Peter.

Mr. Rabbit followed Peter's words with, "Well then, let's quit wasting time and get out of here!"

Out they went, determined to find Sara. The family decided to split up and meet at noon. They would see if anyone had found Sara or at least clues that might lead them to her. Off they went in their groups, looking everywhere. They looked in things, on things, behind things, and even under things.

As Peter and Dan walked around, Peter spied a big, green grasshopper hopping along the white snow. He motioned to Dan. Both boys followed the grasshopper through the snow, thinking how wonderful it would be to catch it for future study.

The grasshopper, unaware Peter and Dan were following him, continued slowly. As the boys followed it, they found some small footprints in the snow, which resembled rabbit tracks. Perhaps they were Sara's.

The boys immediately forgot about the grasshopper, and their minds returned to the problem at hand. Finding Sara!

They followed the footprints and were surprised when they suddenly stopped in the snow. There was no sign of Sara. The boys called Sara's name, hoping for a response.

Sara, lying curled up at the bottom of the hole where she had fallen, heard her name being called. Quickly, she realized it was Dan and Peter calling her. Sara stretched up as high as she could on her back paws and called out as loudly as possible. "Peter! Dan! I'm down here!"

Dan was the first to hear Sara calling and began following the sound toward the hole where Sara was trapped. Peter soon followed his brother, and after Sara called out again, they found the hole in the snow.

Leaning over the edge, Peter asked, "How in the world did you get down there?"

"I fell while hopping through the snow. I didn't even see the hole until it was too late. Please get me out!" wailed Sara.

The boys decided Peter should find the rest of their family and bring them back to the hole while Dan stayed with Sara. Peter finally located his mom, dad, and sisters and led them to Sara and Dan while explaining what had happened.

Although they were interested in how it happened, they were more concerned with making sure Sara was all right and figuring out how to get her out of the hole.

When the family finally arrived, they were all out of breath

"Sara! Are you all right?" gasped Mrs. Rabbit with concern.

"Yes, Mama," Sara responded. "I was beginning to worry, but now that you're all here, I know everything will be just fine."

The entire family tried to think of a way to save Sara, but as small as they all were and as deep as the hole was, they didn't believe they would be able to help at all. The bunnies sat around the hole, trying to think of a way to get her out as fast as possible.

"Sara!" yelled Mr. Rabbit. "Can you see any way of stepping on the side of the hole so you can get higher?"

"No, I don't," replied Sara in a scared, quiet voice.

It's hopeless, they thought, and they all began to cry. The Rabbit Family cried and cried until the forest animals heard them. As they listened, they wondered what could be wrong and why were they crying.

Large and small, the animals of the forest gathered around the area where the cries were coming from. They poked their heads out from behind the trees and rocks to make sure there was no danger, then they cautiously gathered around the Rabbit Family.

"May we be of any help to you?" Freda Fox asked softly, not wanting to startle the family.

"I'm not sure," said Mr. Rabbit. "Our daughter, Sara, has fallen down this man-made trap, and we're just too small to get her out." He wiped tears from his face, hoping no one would notice he, too, had been crying.

"I think we can help if we put our heads together," said Barney Bear. "It's worth a try. What do you think, Mr. and Mrs. Rabbit?"

"Well, it is worth a try, I suppose," said Mr. and Mrs. Rabbit.

All the animals were thinking of ways to save poor little Sara. First, they tried finding some sort of vine to use, but they could not find anything long enough. After trying the longest one they found, Ricky Raccoon thought of an idea. He thought if they couldn't find a long enough vine, maybe they could make one!

If all the animals attached their paws, hands, and tails together, they could make a rope out of their bodies, and Sara could climb out of the trap.

After explaining his idea to the rest of the animals everyone agreed it might just work. They set the plan into motion.

The animals slowly wrapped their paws, hands, and tails together to form a rope. The largest and heaviest animals formed the beginning of the chain. The lighter animals were on the other end, hanging down into the hole.

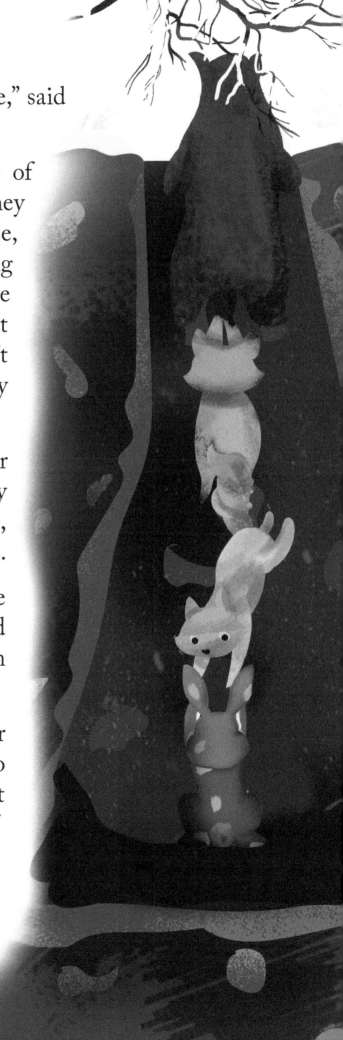

Down and down, further and further, the animals went into the dark, freezing hole to rescue Sara. When they finally reached her, she carefully climbed up the animal chain so the other animals would not lose their grip. When Sara arrived at the top of the hole, she jumped off Barney Bear's shoulders, happy that she had been saved!

Sara thanked everyone and gave her family lots of hugs and kisses. Mr. and Mrs. Rabbit were relieved to see Sara was not injured.

Mrs. Rabbit held Sara in her arms, "We love you, Sara. We are very glad you are all right. I hope you have learned your lesson about wandering off." said Mrs. Rabbit as she kissed Sara's forehead.

Sara answered, "Yes, Mama, I have learned a lesson that I will never ever forget!"

We love you Sara and we are both glad you are all right!

After thanking the animals, Mr. and Mrs. Rabbit gathered their children and herded them home, where they lived happily ever after in their cuddly home in the Gila Forest.

THE END

Ingram Content Group UK Ltd.
Milton Keynes UK
UKHW050936260723
425760UK00003B/78